THE ANGRY MOON

retold by William Sleator, with pictures by Blair Lent

An Atlantic Monthly Press Book

Little, Brown and Company BOSTON TORONTO

The original legend which suggested this story was first recorded by Dr. John R. Swanton in Bulletin 39 of the Bureau of American Ethnology, *Tlingit Myths and Texts* (Washington, D.C.: Government Printing Office, 1909). The illustrations are elaborations on original Tlingit motifs, and are not meant to be authentic.

THE ANGRY MOON

Lupan and Lapowinsa were friends. Always they were together. They spent their days making arrows out of feathers and birch shoots, and walking in the country surrounding their village.

One summer night, they were walking in a large, grassy field. The moon was full, and very bright, and almost seemed to be watching them.

"Look at the moon," said Lapowinsa, laughing. "How ugly it looks with those funny marks all over its face."

"Hush!" whispered Lupan. "You mustn't say things like that about the moon!"

No sooner had he spoken than a huge shadow swept over the field. A strange, shimmering rainbow appeared out of the shadow and settled around Lapowinsa, bathing her in a pale, flickering glow. She cried out in fear. Lupan stepped towards her and the rainbow suddenly vanished, the shadow fell away, and Lupan was standing alone in the moonlight.

Over and over again he called to Lapowinsa, but she was nowhere to be seen. He ran to the top of a little hill in the center of the field, from which he could see all around. The field was empty. "The moon has taken her," he thought, and he sat down on the hill and wept.

When he had no more tears he looked up at the sky and saw a very large, bright star right beside the moon. A strange idea came into his mind. "Perhaps I can hit that star," he said to himself. He took out his bow and arrow, and aiming very carefully, shot at the star. In a moment the star disappeared, and the arrow did not return. Encouraged, he pulled another arrow out of his quiver, for it was packed with all the arrows he and Lapowinsa had made together, and shot it in the same direction. Over and over again, arrow after arrow, he shot at the place where the star had been. None of them fell to the ground.

When almost all the arrows were gone he saw something hanging from the sky, very close to him. It was a chain made of all the arrows he had shot, each one fastened to the other. He shot a few more, until the chain almost reached the ground.

Just as he shot his last arrow the sun began to rise, for it had taken him all night to shoot so many. As the first rays of the sun touched the chain of arrows, it became a ladder, leading up to the sky. For a moment Lupan was stunned with fear and amazement, but he did not hesitate for long. Without knowing why, he picked a few branches from some nearby bushes and stuck them into his hair. And then he stepped onto the ladder.

Up and up he climbed, higher and higher, not daring to stop, not daring to look down. Powerful winds shook the ladder violently, making it swing back and forth in wide, whistling arcs, but he hung on. Driving rains came and beat down on him, making the ladder wet and slippery, but his grip was strong and he did not fall. Night came, and he wrapped himself about the ladder and slept.

The sunlight that woke Lupan the next morning was the brightest he had ever seen. He was stiff and hungry, and his head felt strangely heavy. He put his hand up to find that the branches in his hair had grown to bushes full of big red and blue berries. Again he wondered what had made him put the branches in his hair the day before. He ate the berries, for he was very hungry, and dropped the empty branches down to the earth.

On he climbed, through heavy black clouds and thin white mists, until all the clouds were far below. At nightfall he reached the top of the ladder. Too exhausted to notice what was around him, he lay down and fell asleep.

17

In his sleep he heard a voice saying to him, "Wake up, I am coming for you." He opened his eyes, but could see no one. He closed his eyes again, and soon heard the same voice, saying, "Wake up, I am here." He jumped to his feet, and saw a little boy beside him.

"I have come to take you to my grandmother," said the stranger. "She has been watching you climb here from the earth."

And so Lupan followed the little boy through the sky country until they came to the grandmother's house. The old woman welcomed them, and the three of them sat down around the fire.

"It is I who helped you on your way to this country," said the grandmother. "I could tell that you were brave and had great need to come up into the sky."

"I have come to find Lapowinsa," Lupan said.

"Yes, I know," said the old woman. "She has been captured by the moon, whose house is very near here. We can hear her crying." They listened, and Lupan heard Lapowinsa's voice, wailing as if she were in pain.

"I must go to her!" he cried, jumping up, but the old woman pulled him back.

"Wait," she said. "First you must have food, for you are weak from hunger."

She raised her hand to her mouth, and a roasted fish appeared upon it. She raised it again, and there was a toasted ear of corn. A third time she raised her hand, and it was laden with fresh fruit. Lupan ate hungrily, and soon felt strong and refreshed.

"Now," said the grandmother, "when you go to the house of the moon, you must take four things." She handed him a pine cone, a fish eye, a rose, and a small piece of stone. Then she and the boy wished him good luck, and stood at the door of their house as Lupan hurried away, into the land of the moon.

The closer Lupan got to the house of the moon, the louder Lapowinsa's cries became, and he began to run. Something was sticking out of the smoke hole. As he came closer he saw that it was Lapowinsa's head, and realized with horror that she was caught there and was being scorched by the fire!

He climbed up onto the roof and ran over to her, stepping softly so that the moon could not hear his footsteps. Lapowinsa was so overjoyed to see him that she stopped crying. "Don't stop crying!" he whispered, "The moon mustn't know I am taking you away!" So on she cried as Lupan pulled her out of the smoke hole. He pushed the pine cone into her place, and it began to wail just as she had done. Then, hand in hand, they jumped from the roof and started to run.

But soon the pine cone withered from the heat. It stopped wailing and fell into the fire. The moon realized that he had been tricked and flew into a violent rage.

Thundering from the house, he rolled after Lupan and Lapowinsa much faster than they could run.

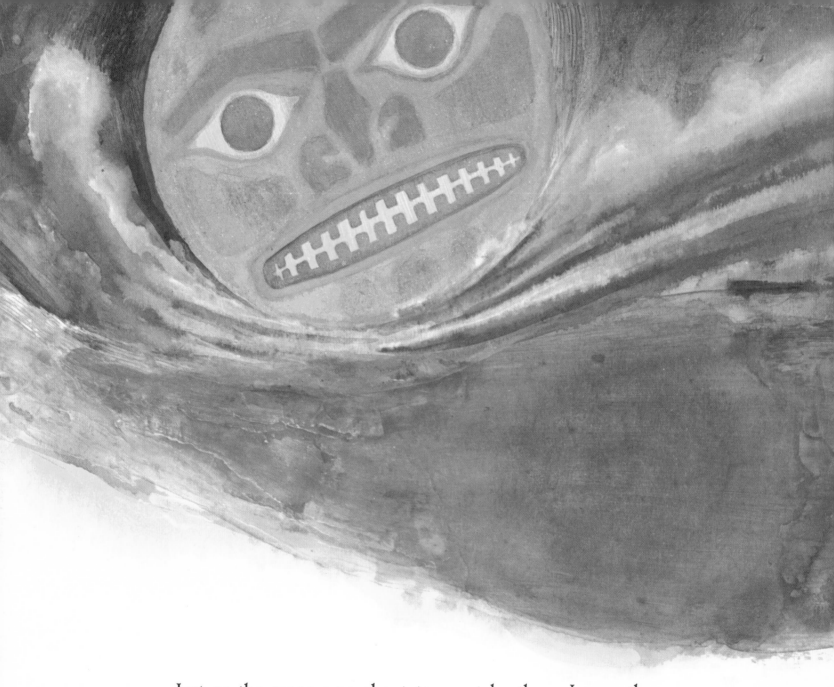

Just as the moon was about to overtake them, Lupan threw
the fish eye behind him, and where it fell a large lake appeared.
The moon could not stop in time and slid into the

water, sending up huge sheets of spray. Cold and wet, he pulled himself out and had to roll all the way around the lake, so that he was far behind them.

The moon traveled so quickly that soon he was right at their heels, and Lupan tossed the rose behind him. Suddenly the moon was caught in a thicket of tangled roses. Struggling and

scratching himself on the thorns, he fought his way through.
When he finally dragged himself out he was mad with fury.
The whole sky shook with his rage, and he rolled even faster.

When they could feel his cold breath upon their necks, Lupan
tossed the little stone behind, and there was a gigantic mountain.
So steep it was that the moon could not climb it, but kept
rolling helplessly up and down, again and again.

Lupan and Lapowinsa reached the grandmother's house, tired
and breathless, but laughing with relief. The old woman and
the child welcomed them, and took them inside to rest. They
thanked the grandmother for all the help she had given them,
but as soon as they were rested they longed to be back on the
earth.

"Your ladder is still there," the grandmother said. "You may
return to the earth whenever you wish."

43

Bidding the old woman and the boy goodbye, Lupan and Lapowinsa walked for the last time across the sky country. Soon they came to the ladder, fading away into the clouds below. They started down carefully, Lupan going first so that he could catch Lapowinsa if she should slip. Slowly they descended, step by step, through thick, puffy clouds that left them glistening with tiny drops of water.

They were so eager to get home that they did not stop to rest. Just as the sun was about to set they reached the earth. As the sun's last rays touched the ladder it became once more a chain of arrows, and clattered to the ground in a heap. The two children happily packed them back into the quiver.

Then Lupan and Lapowinsa ran together into the village, where they were greeted with cries of joy. They led long and happy lives, and people came from miles around to hear their story. It was passed down from one generation to another, and is remembered to this day.